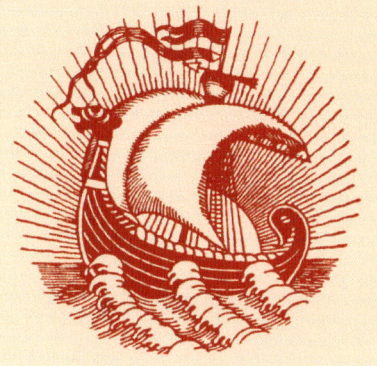

# The Tale of Tsar Saltan

Recorded by Alexander Afanasyev

Illustrations by Ivan Bilibin

THE TALE OF TSAR SALTAN BY ALEXANDER AFANASYEV

Illustrations by Ivan Bilibin
Translation by Post Wheeler

ISBN 978-1-910880-71-5
Published by The Planet, 2019
www.the-planet-books.com

# The Tale of Tsar Saltan

In ancient days, long before our time, in a certain Tsardom of a realm far beyond the blue sea-ocean, there was a Tsar, young in years, named Saltan, who was so handsome and so clever that songs were sung and tales told of him, and beautiful maidens everywhere dreamt of him at night. Minded to rule his Tsardom well, he used to wander forth at dusk in all four directions of his capital, in order to see and hear, and thus he perceived much good and much evil and saw many strange sights. One evening, as he passed the house of a rich merchant, he saw through the window three lovely damsels, the merchant's daughters, sitting at their needlework, and drawing near he overheard their conversation.

The eldest said: "If the Tsar were to wed me, I would grind flour so fine that the like of the bread I would bake from it could not be found in the whole world."

The Tsar, hearing, thought: "That would be good bread truly; however, the bread I eat now is not so bad."

The second said: "If the Tsar were to wed me, I would weave for him a kaftan of gold and silver thread, so that he would shine like the Firebird."

"That would be good weaving, indeed," thought the Tsar; "though little enough need have I for such a splendid coat."

Then the youngest daughter, who was named Marfa, said: "As for me, if the Little Father Tsar became my husband, I know how neither to spin nor to weave, but I would bear him seven hero-sons like bright falcons, that should be the comeliest in his Tsardom; and their legs should be golden to the knee and their arms silver to the elbow, and in their hair should be little stars."

Tsar Saltan, listening, was well pleased with this speech. "Glad would I be to be the father of seven such sons," he said to himself; and returning to his Palace, he summoned his Boyars and Court Ministers, and despatched them to the house

of the merchant to bring his youngest daughter, whom he purposed to make his Tsaritsa. He ordered a great festival and spread tables of oak, at which all the folk of the Tsardom ate, drank and made merry.

On the third day he and the merchant's daughter were married, and slept on an ivory bed, and began to live together, soul with soul, in all joy and contentment. The two elder daughters of the merchant, however, were envious; one sulked over her oven and the other wept over her loom, and both hated their sister because the Tsar had preferred her over them.

Now there was war in those days and whether after a long time or a short time, it became necessary for Tsar Saltan to take the field. When he was depart-

ing, Tsaritsa Marfa wept long and would not be comforted. So Saltan sent for her two sisters to remain with her until his return. And they, although they hated their sister, pretending great love for her, came at once to the Palace. So the Tsar mounted his good horse and, bidding his wife care for herself for his sake, rode away to the fight.

It befell when the Tsar had been three months absent that three babes were born to his Tsaritsa—such lovely little sons that their like cannot be told or described, but can only be imagined, and each had legs golden to the knee, arms silver to the elbow, and little stars in the hair set close together. And Tsaritsa Marfa sent to her husband a fleet messenger to tell him of their birth.

Her sisters, however, kept back the messenger and sent another in his place with this message: "Thy Tsaritsa, our sister, who boasted that she would bear thee Princes of gold and silver, hath borne thee now neither sons nor daughters, but instead, three wretched little kittens."

Then they bribed the nurses and attending women, took from the Tsaritsa, while she slept, the three boy-babies, and put in their jewelled cradles three kittens. As for the beautiful children, they gave them to a Baba Yaga, and the cruel old witch put them into an underground room, in a forest, under a crooked oak tree, whose entrance was closed by a great flat stone.

When the Tsar heard the words of the messenger, he was greatly angered. He sent orders to throw the kittens into the sea-ocean and was minded also to kill his wife. This, however, he could not bear to do, so much did he love her. "I will forgive this fault," he said to himself. "Perchance she may yet give me sons fit for a Tsar."

He returned at length to his Tsardom and lived with his wife happily as before, till there was held a great hunt on the open steppe, and he rode away to kill wild geese and swans. And scarce had he been gone three days, when two more sons were born to his wife, the Tsaritsa Marfa,—such lovely babes that one could not look sufficiently at them—and each had legs golden to the knee, arms silver to the elbow, and little stars in the hair clustering close together.

The Tsaritsa sent in haste for a nurse, and the servant, as it happened, met on his way the old witch. "Where dost thou haste so fast?" she asked him.

"Not far," he replied.

"Tell me instantly," said the Baba Yaga, grinding her teeth, "or it will be the worse for thee!"

"Well," said the servant, "if thou must know, I go to fetch a nurse to the Palace, for two hero-sons have just been born to our mistress, the Tsaritsa."

"Take me as nurse," commanded the witch.

"That I dare not," the servant replied, "lest the Tsar, on his return, strike my head from off my shoulders."

"Obey me," snarled the Baba Yaga, "or meet a worse fate this instant!"

The servant, trembling for his life, returned with the old witch, who, as soon as she came in to the Tsaritsa Marfa, took from her, while she slept, the two lovely babes, put in their place under the sable coverlet two blind puppies, and carried the children to the underground room in the forest. Having done this, she told the two sisters, who, hastening to the Palace, bribed the serving women and despatched a messenger to the Tsar to say: "Our sister, thy Tsaritsa, who boasted that she would bear thee Tsareviches of silver and gold, hath borne thee now neither sons nor daughters, but instead two miserable little puppies."

When the messenger brought him this message, the Tsar's anger waxed hot. He ordered the puppies to be thrown into the sea-ocean, and would have slain his wife but for his great love. However, after his anger had softened, he said to himself: "This second fault also I will pass over. Perchance even yet she will bear me sons fit for a Tsar." And, returning to his capital, he lived happily with her as before.

It happened at length that the Tsar went to a distant Tsardom to pay a visit of ceremony, and this time he set a strong guard about the Palace, with strict command to allow no one whatever to go in or out. When he had been absent six months, two more babes were born to the Tsaritsa—sons of a loveliness that is known only in a tale, with legs golden to the knee, arms silver to the elbow, and with little stars in their hair. And the Tsaritsa, deeming herself safe by reason of the guard about the Palace, bade them peal all the bells for joy.

Hearing the rejoicing, the sisters guessed what had occurred, and sent at once for the Baba Yaga, who by a witch's charm caused a deep sleep to fall upon all the guardsmen so that each slumbered where he stood, and she herself entered the Palace. When the Tsaritsa saw her, however, she hid one of the babes, whom she

had named Guidon, in her sleeve, so that the Baba Yaga, though she carried away the other, did not see it. In place of the babe, the old witch left a piece of wood, and the sisters, as before, bribed the attendants, and sent a messenger to the Tsar to say: "Thy Tsaritsa, our sister, who boasted that she would bear thee sons of gold and silver, hath borne thee now neither son nor daughter, neither is it a frog nor a snake, but a little log of wood."

When the Tsar heard this message, he well-nigh lost his senses in the violence of his rage. After his anger had somewhat subsided, he ordered the log of wood to be thrown into the sea-ocean, and sent a letter to his Prime Minister, bidding him call together his Boyars and Princes of all the Realm to consider the matter on his return.

The messenger rode back with the royal letter, but the two wicked sisters met him on his way, and by stealth stole the letter from his pocket and put in its place another, which read: "I, Tsar Saltan, bid my Boyars without delay to seize the Tsaritsa, put her into a wooden barrel bound with iron, and cast it into the deepest abyss of the sea-ocean."

The messenger delivered the letter, and at once the Boyars came to the Tsaritsa and told her the cruel decree. They pitied her and wept with her, but there was nothing to be done, since the Tsar's will was law, and the same day, with the babe still hidden in her sleeve, she was put into a barrel, and it was thrown into the wide sea-ocean.

Soon after, the Tsar returned, ready, so great was his love, to forgive his wife a third time. But it was then too late, and, thinking that the Tsaritsa was drowned, he at length married the elder of the two sisters, and brought them both to live in his Palace.

Whether the barrel floated a long time or a short time in the sea-ocean, on smooth water or rough water, the little Guidon, who had been hidden in the Tsaritsa's sleeve, was growing like wheat flour when new yeast is added to it, not by days but by hours, until at length he began to speak.

"Little mother," he said, "I have not room enough. Let me stretch myself!"

"Nay, little soul," she answered. "I hear no sound of the waves lapping on the sand. The water is deep beneath us. If thou dost stretch, we shall be drowned."

The barrel floated on and on, and at length its bottom began to scratch against hard pebbles.

Then the little boy said: "We touch something, little mother. May I stretch myself?"

She gave him permission, and he began to stretch himself, and so strong and sturdy was he that the iron bands broke asunder and the barrel fell to pieces. Looking about them, they saw that they were on an island, which had a high hill, sloping down to a green field, surrounded by a forest. The mother and her son crossed the field and entered the forest, searching for a path that should lead them to some habitation. They found none, however, and were about to return wearied to the meadow, when Tsarevich Guidon came upon a purse lying on the ground.

11

Opening it, they found a flint and steel, and were glad, thinking that with a fire they could protect themselves against cold and wild beasts. Tsarevich Guidon struck the flint and steel together, when instantly there appeared a sharp axe and a huge hammer.

"Here we are, Master," said the axe and hammer. "By God's blessing, what command wilt thou be pleased to lay upon us?"

"Build us a Palace to live in," answered Guidon, "and fetch us food and drink."

At once the axe flew at the trees and began to chop, square, and sharpen them, and the hammer to pound them into the earth for a foundation; and while the Tsaritsa and the Tsarevich watched, there began to rise on the edge of the forest a Palace of white stone, with battlemented walls, more splendid than has ever been seen in any Tsardom, richer than can be guessed or imagined, whose like can neither be told in speech nor written in a tale.

They entered it, and found therein whatever the soul could ask.

Now, before many days it befell that a ship came sailing that way, and the shipmen wondered greatly to see there, on what had been an uninhabited island, a stately Palace, with golden domes and walls of white stone, and they landed to see this marvel.

The Tsaritsa met them and made them her guests, giving them food and drink to their hearts' desire.

"O merchants," she said, "in what trade are ye concerned, and whither sail ye from here?"

They answered: "We have traded in the skins of sables and black foxes in foreign marts; now we sail to the east, to the Tsardom of Tsar Saltan the Glorious."

"A happy voyage to you," said the Tsaritsa, "and give a greeting from me to Tsar Saltan."

The merchants re-embarked and sailed to the Tsardom of Tsar Saltan, who called them to be his guests; and they came before him, where he sat sad-faced on his golden throne, with his new wife and her sister by his side. As they sat at table, the Tsar said: "O merchants and tradesmen! Have ye voyaged far, and to what lands went ye? Is it well or ill across the blue sea-ocean? And what new wonder is there in the white world?"

The shipmen replied: "O Tsar's Majesty! We travelled over all the world, and were on our way hither when we saw a new wonder more marvellous than any. There has been of old time in the sea-ocean an island, without inhabitants, save they were wizards or wild beasts. It had a great flat meadow on which grew a single oak tree, and about it was a dense forest. So hath it always been; yet but now, as we came to it, we found there a splendid Palace, with towers whose tops were golden, and with green gardens about it. In it dwells a beautiful Tsaritsa and a Tsarevich, and the Tsarevich has legs golden to the knee, and arms silver to the elbow, and in his hair are little stars. We landed there, and the Tsaritsa entertained us royally, and sent a greeting to thee."

Tsar Saltan wondered greatly to hear, and said: "As God lets me live, I will visit this wonderful island and see it with my own eyes." But his wicked wife and her younger sister, not wishing him to go, began to sneer.

"A Palace on an island! What is that to be compared to a marvel of which I can tell thee?"

"What marvel is that?" asked the Tsar.

She answered: "Across three times nine countries, in the thirtieth Tsardom, there is a green garden, and in the garden is a mill which grinds of itself. It winnows the grain and throws the chaff a hundred versts away. By the mill stands a golden column, and up and down the column climbs a learned cat. As it goes up it sings songs, and as it comes down it tells stories."

Hearing of this new wonder, the Tsar gave up his purpose to visit the island.

The merchants, having loaded their ship with other goods, sailed on a second voyage, and, passing the Tsaritsa's island, cast anchor, and were again entertained; and they recounted there how Tsar Saltan had desired to sail thither till his wife had told him of the mill, the golden column, and the story-telling cat.

As soon as they had made their farewells and sailed away, Tsarevich Guidon took from the purse the flint and steel, and struck them sharply together, and immediately the axe and the hammer appeared, saying: "Here we are, thy servants! By God's blessing, what dost thou bid us do?"

"I will have, near this Palace," said the Tsarevich, "a mill which grinds and winnows of itself and throws the chaff a hundred versts away. By it must be a column of gold on which climbs a cat, telling tales and singing songs."

At once the axe and hammer disappeared, and, next morning, when he went to his balcony, the Tsarevich saw that the garden, the mill, the golden column, and the clever cat had all been brought as he had commanded.

He caused his servants, the axe and hammer, to build by the column a crystal summer house, in which the cat should live, and each day the Tsaritsa and Tsarevich Guidon amused themselves by listening to its songs and stories.

Time passed, and again the ship returned from her voyage, and the merchants wondered to see the new marvels. They landed, and the Tsaritsa, meeting them, bade them enter and taste of her hospitality. She gave them honey to eat and milk to drink, and treated them so handsomely that they scarce knew themselves for

15

pleasure. "O tradesmen," she asked them, "what do ye barter, and whither sail ye from here?"

"We have bartered carpets and stallions from the Don river around the whole world," they answered. "Now we sail to the eastward, to the Tsardom of Tsar Saltan the Mighty."

"A good journey to you," said the Tsaritsa. "Bear to Tsar Saltan greeting from my son, Tsarevich Guidon."

The merchants spread sail and voyaged to the Tsardom of Tsar Saltan, and a second time he summoned them to bear him company. And as they ate and drank in his sumptuous hall, he asked them: "O tradesmen and mariners, doubtless ye have traversed the whole earth. What have ye seen, and what news do ye bear? And is there any new marvel in the white world?"

They answered: "O mighty Tsar Saltan! we have truly visited many countries and seen many strange things, but the most wonderful is this. When we were thy guests before, we told thee of an island on which, bare and uninhabited of old, we found a splendid Palace with a beautiful Tsaritsa and a brave Tsarevich. On this sailing we passed again that way and put in at the island, and now beside the Palace of white stone there is a green garden with a mill that grinds and winnows of itself and casts the chaff a hundred versts away. Beside it, is a golden column on which a cat climbs continually up and down, singing songs and telling tales. And there is a summer house of crystal in which the cat lives. The Tsaritsa showed us these wonders, and her son, Tsarevich Guidon, sends a greeting to thee."

When Tsar Saltan heard this, again was he seized with a desire to see the island, but, as before, his evil wife and her sister sneered, and the wife said:

"A rare thing in truth! Thinkest thou the mill and cat are so wonderful? What, indeed, are they beside a marvel of which I know?"

"What is that?" asked the Tsar.

She answered: "Across three times nine lands, in the thirtieth Tsardom, there is a wood and in the wood a fir tree. On the tree lives a squirrel, cracking nuts with its teeth. These are not ordinary nuts, for their shells are of gold and the kernels of emerald. He who owns this wonder is the richest Tsar in all the world, for his wealth never ceases to increase until it cannot be reckoned."

And, deeming this an even greater marvel, Tsar Saltan again laid by his purpose to visit the island.

The merchants filled their ship with new merchandise and set sail for distant lands and, passing the island again, were welcomed by Tsaritsa Marfa and Tsarevich Guidon, to whom they recounted their visit to Tsar Saltan. Nor did they fail to tell how he had purposed to sail thither until he had heard of the fir tree, the squirrel and the nuts of gold and emerald.

When they had departed, Tsarevich Guidon struck together his flint and steel, and the axe and hammer, appearing, said: "Master, we are here! By God's blessing, what wilt thou that we accomplish?"

"Plant me here," said the Tsarevich, "a fir tree. On it let there be a squirrel which cracks with its teeth nuts whose shells are of gold and their kernels of emerald."

The axe and hammer disappeared and next day, when he arose, the Tsarevich found all done as he had commanded. He bade them build a summer house of crystal for the squirrel to live in, and the golden shells and emeralds he put into the Palace treasury till the wealth could not be reckoned.

It befell at length that the merchants' ship returned from its voyage and cast anchor at the island. The Tsaritsa met and welcomed them, giving them to eat and drink till for rich feasting they scarce remembered their names. "O shipmen and merchants," she said, "what merchandise do ye bear and whither fare ye from here?"

They answered: "We are laden with steel swords and with precious armour which we have traded through the whole world, and our way is eastward, to the Tsardom of Tsar Saltan the Magnificent."

"A fair wind to you," said the Tsaritsa. "Carry my greeting, and that of my son Guidon, to Tsar Saltan."

So they sailed on to the Tsar's dominions and a third time were summoned to his presence.

They sat at table and feasted; and before they left him, he said: "O merchants and travellers, in all your wayfaring what new sights have ye seen? And is there any fresh marvel in the white world?"

"O Tsar's Majesty!" they replied. "We told thee before of the island with its Palace, its self-grinding mill, its golden column and its learned cat. On this voyage also we visited it and were entertained right royally. And now, in addition to the other wonders we recounted, there is a fir tree, on which sits a squirrel, cracking with its teeth nuts, whose shells are gold and whose kernels are emerald. The squirrel lives in a crystal summer house, and the gold and emeralds are piled in the Palace treasury till it overflows with such riches that the like is surely not to be seen in the whole world. The noble Tsarevich Guidon showed us these things, and we bear to thee a greeting from him and from the Tsaritsa, his mother."

The Tsar was astonished to hear of this and said to his wife: "In truth, the wonders of which thou hast told me are all to be found in this surpassing island. Canst thou recall any marvel to match this?"

18

She answered spitefully: "That is not so hard. There is in a dense forest, under a crooked oak tree, a great flat stone which covers an underground room, and in the room are six Tsareviches, more beautiful than can be told. Each has legs golden to the knee, arms silver to the elbow, and in his hair are little stars. A witch keeps them hidden, and there lives in the white world no man clever enough to find them out or to learn who they are."

Tsar Saltan, hearing, was silent, thinking of his dead wife and of her promise to bear him such hero-sons. He dismissed the merchants with rich gifts, and they bought goods to fill their ships and sailed away again on the wide sea-ocean.

In time they touched at the island of Tsaritsa Marfa, and, being entertained, recounted to her their visit to Tsar Saltan's Court and told how, for a third time, he had purposed to voyage thither, until his wife had told of the underground room and of the six Tsareviches with legs golden, arms of silver, and with stars in their hair.

When the shipmen had departed on their way, Tsaritsa Marfa told Tsarevitch Guidon the story of her life with Tsar Saltan and what she had suffered at the hands of her wicked sisters. "These six Tsareviches," she said, "whom the witch hides in the forest, are surely none other than my own dear sons and thy little brothers. Let us depart to search for them."

So the Tsarevich struck together his flint and steel and bade the axe and hammer build a ship which would fly either on land or sea and which should take them to the witch's forest. Next morning all was ready, and they straightway embarked and sailed over the sea-ocean, and over the open steppe to the edge of the forest, where the Baba Yaga had hidden the stolen Princes.

Whether the journey was long or short, whether it took a twelvemonth or a day, they found the crooked oak tree and the Tsarevich lifted the great flat stone, and they entered the underground room. They looked here and there and presently saw six little soiled shirts lying on chairs. The Tsaritsa took them, washed them clean, rinsed, wrung and hung them to dry. Six little plates sat on a table unwashed. She washed them all and dried them and swept the floor. Hearing a noise outside, she said: "Someone is coming. Let us hide behind the stove."

They hid themselves, and the six Tsareviches entered, all with legs golden to the knee, arms silver to the elbow, and with little stars in their hair. They saw how the room had been swept and the plates and shirts made clean, and were glad. "Show thyself," they cried, "thou who hast washed and tidied our house. If thou art a beautiful girl, thou shalt be our little sister, and if thou art a Tsaritsa, thou shalt be our little mother!"

Then Tsaritsa Marfa showed herself, and the six Tsareviches ran to her, and she took them in her arms and kissed and caressed them and told them who they were—that she was indeed their mother and Tsarevich Guidon their little brother. She brought them from the forest to the magic ship, and it sailed with them like a white swan, over the open steppe and the blue sea-ocean to the Tsaritsa's island, to her Palace of white stone, and there they began to live happily together.

Now when its voyage was finished, the ship of the merchants came back from the ends of the world and put in at the island. The Tsaritsa welcomed them and she and her seven sons gave them such feasts and amusements that for delight they would have remained there forever. "O merchant-travellers," she asked them, "in what cargoes do ye traffic, and whither go ye from here?"

"We have sailed about the whole world," they answered, "with goods of every sort that tradesmen carry, and from here our course lies eastward to the Tsardom of Tsar Saltan the Splendid."

"Fair weather to you," she said, "and take a greeting to Tsar Saltan from me and from my seven sons."

The ship departed, and when it was come to the Tsardom of Tsar Saltan, he made the merchants yet again his guests. And as they ate and drank and made merry, he said to them: "O tradesmen and far-journeying adventurers, ye have sailed to the uttermost lands. What strange thing have ye seen, and is there any new wonder in the white world?"

"O great Tsar Saltan!" they replied, "thou didst hear from us before of the island in the blue sea-ocean, of its Tsaritsa and her Tsarevich, and their Palace of white stone, with the marvels there to be seen. On our way hither we again stopped there, and now the lady hath with her not one Tsarevich but seven, so handsome that we know no words to tell thee of them, and each has legs golden to the knee and arms silver to the elbow, and in their hair are little stars set close together. And when we departed, the Tsaritsa sent to thee greeting from herself and these seven sons."

When the merchants spoke thus, the wicked wife of Tsar Saltan opened her mouth to speak, but the Tsar rose up and silenced her.

"Tell me no more of thy marvels," he said to her. "What am I, a Tsar or a child?" And having dismissed the merchants with presents, he sent for his Ministers and Boyars, and bade a fleet to be prepared and the same day set sail for the island.

Tsarevich Guidon, sitting with his brothers at the window, saw the ships of Tsar Saltan coming over the blue sea-ocean, and called to his mother, "See, our little father is coming!" He went to meet him and brought him into the Palace to the Tsaritsa.

Seeing her, Tsar Saltan recognized her, and his breath stopped and his face flowed with tears. He kissed her and embraced his seven sons and all began to weep and rejoice together.

When they had spent some days in such happiness, they went aboard the ships and sailed back to Tsar Saltan's realm. He summoned his Ministers and Boyars, his Princes and Judges, and they condemned his evil wife, and she and her sister were put into a chest barred and bound with iron, and the chest was thrown into the sea-ocean. But God did not protect them as He had protected the Tsaritsa and her son, for they sank at once into the lowest abyss and were drowned.

But Tsar Saltan and Tsaritsa Marfa, with the seven Tsareviches, lived always together in bright-faced joy, and increased in all good things. And Tsaritsa Marfa was as beautiful in her old age as she had been in her youth.

Printed in Great Britain
by Amazon